POKÉMON ™

Island of the Giant Pokémon

ISBN 0-439-10466-1

©1995, 1996, 1998 Nintendo, Creatures, Game Freak.
TM & ® are trademarks of Nintendo.
©1999 Nintendo.

Published by Scholastic Inc.
SCHOLASTIC and associated logos are trademarks
and/or registered trademarks of Scholastic Inc.

12 11 10 9 8 7 6 5   9/9 0 1 2 3 4/0

Printed in the U.S.A.

First Scholastic printing, July 1999

POKÉMON™

Island of the Giant Pokémon

Adapted by Tracey West

SCHOLASTIC INC.
New York   Toronto   London   Auckland   Sydney
Mexico City   New Delhi   Hong Kong

There are more books
about Pokémon.

Collect them all!

#1 I Choose You!

#2 Island of the Giant Pokémon

coming soon

#3 Attack of the Prehistoric Pokémon

Pokémon

Theme Song

I want to be the very best,
Like no one ever was.
To catch them is my real test,
To train them is my cause.
I will travel across the land,
Searching far and wide.
Each Pokémon, to understand
The power that's inside
Pokémon
(Gotta catch 'em all)
It's you and me
I know it's my destiny
Pokémon!
You're my best friend
In a world we must defend
Pokémon
(Gotta catch 'em all)
A heart so true
Our courage will pull us through
You teach me and I'll teach you
Pokémon
(Gotta catch 'em all)
Gotta catch 'em all
Pokémon

Pokémon Theme
Words and Music by Tamara Loeffler and John Siegler
Copyright © 1998 Pikachu Music (BMI)
Worldwide rights for Pikachu Music administered by Cherry River Music Co. (BMI)
All Rights Reserved   Used By Permission

luck catching new Pokémon. But his luck changed when he met Misty and Brock. They were Pokémon trainers, too, and they had taught him a lot.

Ash looked down at the five red-and-white balls that were attached to his belt. They were Poké Balls, and his captured Pokémon stayed inside the balls — until Ash needed them.

"I started out with empty Poké Balls," Ash said. "And now they're filled with Pokémon."

"Right!" Misty said. "You've got a Bulbasaur." Bulbasaur was blue-green and had a plant bulb on its back.

"And there's Squirtle," Brock said. Squirtle was a Water Pokémon that looked like a cute turtle.

"I have a Charmander, too," Ash said, picturing the red Fire Pokémon in his mind. "And don't forget Butterfree." This flying Pokémon looked like a giant butterfly.

1

Cruising for Trouble

"Ash, I can't believe how many Pokémon you've captured so far," Misty said, her red ponytail bobbing on top of her head.

"You've done great," Brock agreed. "You've come a long way since you first began your Pokémon journey."

Ash blushed a little at the praise of his two friends. He had begun his Pokémon training on his tenth birthday. Now he was traveling around the country searching for Pokémon, creatures with amazing powers.

In the beginning, Ash hadn't had much

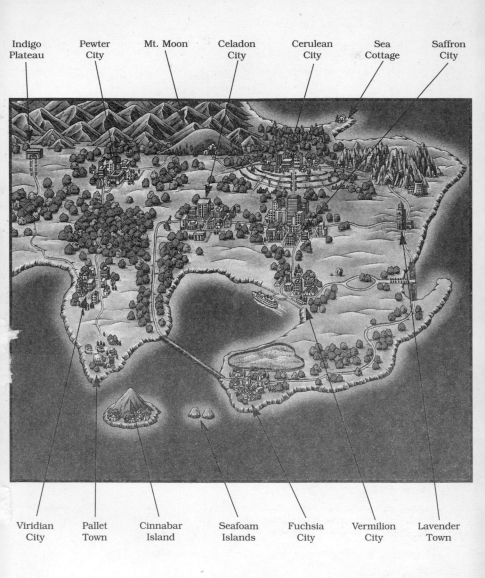

Indigo
Plateau

Pewter
City

Mt. Moon

Celadon
City

Cerulean
City

Sea
Cottage

Saffron
City

Viridian
City

Pallet
Town

Cinnabar
Island

Seafoam
Islands

Fuchsia
City

Vermilion
City

Lavender
Town

Ash always got excited thinking about all of his Pokémon. "And of course there's —"

"*Pi!*" A tiny voice interrupted him.

Ash laughed and picked up the lightning mouse Pokémon at his feet. This Pokémon was bright yellow, with long, pointy ears. It had brown stripes on its back, and its tail was shaped like a lightning bolt.

"Don't worry, Pikachu," Ash said. "You were my very first Pokémon. I could never forget you."

"*Pika!*" Pikachu said happily.

Pikachu jumped on Ash's back. Unlike most other Pokémon, Pikachu didn't stay inside a Poké Ball.

"I wonder what kind of Pokémon we'll see aboard the S.S. *Anne*?" Brock wondered.

"I can't wait to find out!" Ash said. He looked up at the large white cruise ship in front of them. The ocean liner looked like it was as long as a city block and almost as tall as a skyscraper.

"The S.S. *Anne* is such an awesome ship!" Misty said. "I can't believe we're going to take a cruise on her."

"For Pokémon trainers only," Brock said. "It's the chance of a lifetime."

"You can say that again," Ash said. "It seems too good to be true. I can't believe those teenage girls gave us free tickets."

Misty grabbed Ash's sleeve. "Who cares how we got the tickets? Let's get on board!"

Not far away, two teenage girls — a blond and a redhead — watched Ash and his friends board the ship. The blond girl ripped off a wig to reveal short purple hair. It wasn't a teenage girl at all. It was James, one half of a pair of Pokémon thieves called Team Rocket.

"Don't I make the coolest girl," James said in a fake squeaky voice.

The redhead frowned. It was Jessie, James's partner in crime. "Don't be an ignoramus, James. We've got to go talk to the boss."

Jessie and James ran to a nearby lighthouse. They climbed the long, spiral staircase until they reached a small dark room. Meowth, their catlike Pokémon, was fiddling with the knobs of a small control board.

"We got a call from the boss," Meowth said.

A large screen on the wall lit up. The dark figure of a man appeared, his face hidden by shadows.

"Have you handed out all the tickets to the Pokémon cruise?" Giovanni's deep voice was altered by a computer.

"Yes," Jessie said.

"Excellent!" Giovanni said. "My men have already secretly boarded the S.S. *Anne.* When I give them the signal, they will take the Pokémon from all of the trainers we tricked into boarding the ship."

"That's the boss for you! A real genius!" Meowth purred.

Giovanni leaned in closer to the camera. "This time," he said menacingly, "failure is out of the question!"

2

Butterfree VS. Raticate

"What an amazing ship," Ash said, gazing around the S.S. *Anne*.

Ash, Misty, Brock, and Pikachu walked along the ship's deck. They followed a steward in a navy-blue jacket.

"This way to the main hall," he said, directing them to two open doors.

Ash gasped when he stepped inside the hall. The large room was crowded with Pokémon trainers talking excitedly and showing off their Pokémon. Booths lined the walls of the hall, selling everything from Pokémon toys and jewelry to real Pokémon.

"This is like a giant Pokémon convention!" Ash exclaimed.

Misty nodded. "Everyone here is a Pokémon trainer."

Ash looked around the hall. There was so much to do, he wasn't sure where to start. Then loud cheering erupted from the middle of the hall where a crowd had formed a circle. Ash pushed his way through the crowd.

A Pokémon trainer was holding up a Poké Ball. He was a tall man, much older than Ash. The man wore a top hat, a black dinner jacket, a red bow tie, and blue-tinted sunglasses.

The man turned to the crowd. "Is anyone brave enough to challenge my Raticate?"

Ash's heart beat with excitement. Battling your Pokémon against other trainers' Pokémon was something every good Pokémon trainer was taught to do. Ash was itching for a battle.

Ash ran up to the older trainer. "I will!"

Ash knew just which Pokémon he would use, too. "How about battling my Butterfree?"

"As you wish," the man replied. He threw his Poké Ball into the air. "Poké Ball, go!" he cried. Raticate, a large ratlike Pokémon with four sharp fangs, appeared in a blaze of white light.

Ash threw a Poké Ball. "Butterfree, I choose you!"

Butterfree burst from its Poké Ball. Its blue wings flapped in the air. Although it looked like a simple butterfly, Ash knew it was a powerful Pokémon. With its wings spread, the Butterfree was about three feet wide.

Misty, Brock, and Pikachu watched the battle begin.

"Raticate! Tail Whip!" yelled the man.

"Butterfree! Tackle!" Ash yelled.

Raticate jumped into the air. Butterfree flew right at it. The two Pokémon collided in the air. Neither one seemed hurt by the crash. The two Pokémon kept at it. They charged at each other again and again, but neither one seemed weakened.

"Does Ash's Butterfree even stand a chance against that Raticate?" Misty asked nervously.

"Sure," Brock said. "It's a good match. Ash knows what he's doing."

Now the older trainer was changing his strategy.

"Finish it, Raticate! Hyper Fang Attack!" he ordered.

Raticate leaped at Butterfree. Its mouth was wide open, revealing its sharp white fangs. Butterfree dodged the attack just in time.

Ash thought fast. He needed a move that would stop the Raticate in its tracks.

"Butterfree, Stun Spore!" Ash called out.

Butterfree flapped its wings furiously. Shimmering gold spores floated down from its body. The spores covered Raticate. Raticate crashed to the ground, stunned. The spores had paralyzed it!

Ash grew excited. Victory was just a move away.

"Butterfree! Whirlwind!"

But before Butterfree could start the

move, the older trainer stepped inside the battle ring that had been marked out on the floor.

"That's enough!" he said.

"What do you mean?" Ash asked. Competitions between trainers are officially over when one trainer's Pokémon faints.

Ash never ended a battle this way before.

"Let's call it a draw," the man said. He quickly picked up his Raticate.

"But I was winning," Ash said lamely as the man walked away.

Ash recalled Butterfree and put the Poké Ball back on his belt loop. He found Misty, Brock, and Pikachu on the side.

"Nice match," Brock said. "But that trainer was kind of strange."

Misty sneered. "I think he's a coward," she said. "He knew he was going to lose."

Ash shrugged. "It was a good battle. I'm really proud of Butterfree."

"Pikachu," Pikachu called out. The Pokémon was pointing to a buffet table laden with food.

"Good idea. I'm hungry, too," Ash said.

The ship's horn blared as the friends piled food on their plates. Ash spotted an empty table and they sat down. As they ate, Ash could feel the S.S. *Anne* move through the water.

"All right!" Ash said. "We're cruising now."

Misty nudged Ash with her elbow.

"What the —" Ash looked up. The older trainer was approaching the table. At his side was a tall woman with auburn hair piled high on top of her head. She wore a fancy red evening gown.

"That Butterfree of yours is quite extraordinary," the man said.

"It's incredible," the woman agreed.

"Beautiful," said Brock, blushing bright red. Brock was quiet and pretty calm most of the time — except when a beautiful woman was around. Then it was like he was on another planet.

The man didn't seem to notice Brock. "What did you think of my Raticate?" he asked Ash.

"It looked great and it put up a really tough fight," Ash said.

The man stared at Ash through his blue-tinted glasses. "In that case, why don't we trade?"

"Trade Pokémon?" Ash had never heard of that before.

"When people find that they like each other's Pokémon, they trade," the man said.

"It's quite a common practice everywhere."

"Everywhere?" Ash turned to Brock for guidance. Brock was older and more experienced. He knew more about these things than Ash did.

"Should I trade, Brock?" Ash asked.

Brock wasn't listening. He was still blushing at the trainer's beautiful companion. "Sure, Ash. You gotta trade. Everybody should trade," he said absentmindedly.

"Trading is one of the best things about having Pokémon," the man continued.

Ash wasn't sure what to do. He couldn't imagine giving up one of his Pokémon. Especially Butterfree! He had trained and evolved it himself from the time it was a Caterpie. But if everyone did it . . . he didn't want to be different from the other trainers. And Brock said it was all right.

"Well, okay," Ash said.

"Splendid! Follow me," the man said.

Ash and Pikachu followed the man outside the main hall. The man opened the door to a cabin. Inside the small room was a curious-looking machine. There was a silver table with buttons in the front. On top of the table was a kind of screen with two metal tubes extending from either side. The tubes hung down over the table.

The trainer took a Poké Ball and placed it under one of the tubes.

"Put Butterfree's ball under the other tube," the man instructed.

Ash obeyed. The man pressed a red button. Sparks flashed from the ends of the tubes. Then the two Poké Balls were sucked into the tubes. The screen flashed brightly. Ash watched as an image of Butterfree crossed the screen into the man's tube. An image of Raticate crossed the screen into Ash's tube. Then the Poké Balls dropped out of the tubes again.

"It's done," the man said. "Raticate is your new Pokémon."

Ash held the Poké Ball in his hand. Raticate was inside. Raticate was a powerful Pokémon, too. It was kind of cool to have a Raticate.

The man tipped his top hat to Ash and

walked away, carrying the Poké Ball with Butterfree inside.

"Pikachu, did I do the right thing?" he asked softly.

"Pika," Pikachu said sadly.

Ash stared at the Poké Ball in his hand. "I'm not sure, either."

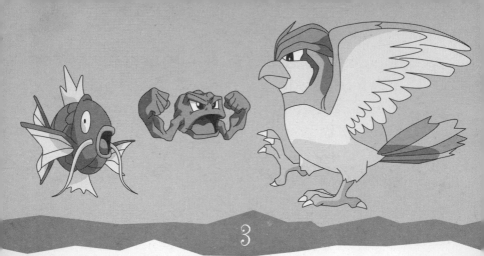

Battle Aboard the S.S. Anne

The S.S. *Anne* glided through the ocean water. In a dark corner of the ocean liner, Team Rocket was about to have a showdown.

"Look what I bought from a Pokémon vendor," James was saying. He held up a gold Poké Ball. "It's a very valuable Pokémon."

James pushed a button on the ball. A fish Pokémon with a gaping mouth appeared. The orange Pokémon flapped its fins in the air. Its big round eyes bulged out of its head.

"It's a Magikarp," James said proudly.

Jessie's green eyes flashed with rage. "You fool. You've been tricked! Magikarp can't do anything but flop around."

"But I couldn't have been tricked. I paid next month's salary to get it," James protested. "Yours, too, Jessie."

"You what?" Jessie screamed.

"*Meowth!* That's enough." Team Rocket's catlike Pokémon stepped in. "We've got work to do!"

Back in the main hall, the Pokémon trainers were talking and shopping at the booths. But not Ash. He was slouched in a corner, staring at the Poké Ball that once held Butterfree.

Misty noticed that Ash looked sad. "What's the matter?" she asked him.

"I was just wondering if that guy is going to take good care of my Butterfree," Ash said.

Misty put a hand on his shoulder.

"Just as I was trading it I remembered the time when it evolved into a Butterfree," Ash continued.

"I remember," Misty said. "First you caught Caterpie. That was the first Pokémon you ever caught on your own."

An image of the green buglike Pokémon flashed through Ash's mind. "That's right. Then Caterpie evolved into Metapod. And when Butterfree hatched out of Metapod, it was so amazing. Butterfree was really special."

"I'm sure Butterfree will —" Misty began, but she was interrupted by a loud slamming sound.

"*Pika?*" Pikachu asked with concern.

Ash looked around the hall. All of the

doors closed automatically. Eight soldiers in black uniforms stormed through the hall. They wore helmets, goggles, and each one had a large square machine strapped to his back. On the front of each uniform was a red letter "R."

That red "R" could only mean one thing, Ash knew. "Team Rocket!" he cried.

The lights went off, plunging the room into darkness. Then a spotlight shone on a table in the center of the hall.

Jessie, James, and Meowth were standing on the table. Glaring at the Pokémon trainers, Jessie and James shouted out their battle cry.

"To protect the world from devastation.
To unite all peoples within our nation.
To denounce the evils of truth and love.
To extend our reach to the stars above.
Jessie!
James!
Team Rocket! Blast off at the speed of
   light!
Surrender now or prepare to fight!"

"*Meowth!* That's right!" added Meowth.

Jessie and James also wore square machines on their backs. Each machine had a hose attached on both sides. James grabbed a hose in each hand.

"Team Rocket will now take possession of your Pokémon," he said, sneering.

James pushed a button on the end of each hose. Jessie and the Team Rocket soldiers did the same. A huge sucking sound filled the hall. The hoses were powerful suction devices. Poké Balls began flying off the trainers' belts. The hoses were going to suck them up!

Ash grabbed a Poké Ball from his belt and held on tightly. "We've got to fight back!" he said.

A boy about Ash's age nodded in agreement. "We can't just surrender!" He threw a Poké Ball at one of the Team Rocket soldiers. A Squirtle appeared in a blaze of light. But the suction power of the hoses was too strong for the Pokémon. Squirtle struggled helplessly against the pull.

"Our Pokémon are too weak," Ash said.

"Not if we have them fight together!" Brock suggested.

Pikachu looked angry. *"Pikachu!"* The air filled with Pikachu's cry. The other Pikachu in the hall came running to Ash's Pikachu. They formed a pyramid.

"PIKACHU!" they cried. Together the Pikachu created a huge electric charge. The air sizzled as they sent a giant Thunderbolt hurling at two Team Rocket soldiers. The soldiers were thrown to the ground, their

bodies shaking from the shock.

"Six more to go," Ash said. He threw the Poké Ball that was in his hand. "Charmander, I choose you," he cried.

The orange Fire Pokémon popped out of the ball. It had a body like a lizard, but it walked on two feet. A red-and-yellow flame blazed on the end of its tail.

Taking Ash's cue, other trainers in the hall released their Charmander. These Pokémon also formed a pyramid. The hall filled with heat as the Charmander combined their powers to create a ball of blue flame. They hurled the fireball at two more of the soldiers.

"Aaaaaaargh!" the soldiers screamed. The fire blast sent them hurtling against a wall. They fell to the ground in a heap, charred from the heat.

"My turn," said Brock, reaching for a Poké Ball. "Geodude, go!"

At Brock's command a Rock Pokémon appeared from the ball. Geodude looked like a big, gray rock with two strong arms. More Geodude bounced along the floor to join Brock's Geodude. The Pokémon held hands and formed a circle around two more Team Rocket soldiers. They began to spin around and around in a circle. They whirled faster and faster. The speed created a tornado wind that sent the two goons flying across the hall.

Next, the trainer in the top hat threw a Poké Ball. "Butterfree, go!"

Butterfree appeared and flew over the

last two soldiers. More Butterfree were flying across the hall to help. The Butterfree flapped their wings, covering the soldiers with golden spores.

Ash detached a Poké Ball from his belt. "Butterfree, go!" he cried.

But a furry Pokémon appeared from the ball. "*Raticate!*" it said.

Ash couldn't believe it. How could he forget? He didn't have a Butterfree anymore.

"I have to get Butterfree back," Ash cried.

Misty grabbed his arm. "We've got bigger things to worry about," she said. "Look!"

The Team Rocket soldiers were weakened by the Pokémon attacks, but they were still tough. All eight were back on their feet and advancing toward the trainers.

"It's time we took care of these guys once and for all," Ash said. He grabbed another Poké Ball from his belt. "Pidgeotto, I choose you!"

A Pokémon that looked like a large, brown-and-white bird burst from the ball. Soon the air was filled with the flapping wings of dozens of Pidgeotto.

"Pidgeotto Group Gust!" Ash called.

The Pidgeotto formed a circle and began to flap their wings. The birdlike Pokémon flapped furiously. A funnel-shaped wind formed that was much faster and stronger than what the group of Geodude had made.

A small tornado formed in the middle of the hall. It spun up to the ceiling. *Crash!* The strong winds blasted a hole in the top of the ship. Ash could see the sky through the hole.

"Pikachu! All together! Thundershock!"

Ash's Pikachu and the other Pikachu in the hall formed another pyramid. The Pokémon began to glow with yellow electric energy. The charge grew. Suddenly, the Pikachu focused the charge, sending a blast like a lightning bolt at the Team Rocket soldiers.

"PIKACHU!" they shouted.

The bolt sent the soldiers flying up, up into the ceiling. They flew through the hole and vanished from sight.

The Pokémon trainers cheered.

"We did it!" Ash said. "We should be

proud of our Pokémon. We taught Team Rocket a lesson they'll never forget."

"Speaking of Team Rocket," Misty said. "Where did they go?"

Ash looked around the hall. They had defeated the Team Rocket soldiers. But where were Jessie, James, and Meowth?

"I'm sure somebody took care of them," Ash said. "I'll look for them later. Right now, I've got to get back my Butterfree!"

4

That Sinking Feeling

Ash approached the trainer in the top hat. "We need to talk," Ash said firmly. He was prepared to battle if he had to.

"What's this about?" the man asked.

"I really want my Butterfree back," Ash explained. "I worked hard training and raising it. Butterfree means a lot to me."

The man had a serious look on his face. Ash tensed, ready to fight. Then the trainer's face softened. "I understand what it's like to care about your Pokémon. Follow me to the Pokémon trading room."

Ash breathed a sigh of relief. This trainer was a little weird, but he wasn't mean. Ash was going to get Butterfree back! Ash followed the trainer into the room. He and the man put their Poké Balls on the machine. The man pushed a button.

The screen lit up, and Ash happily watched as the image of Butterfree crossed

the screen into his Poké Ball. He was so happy he didn't notice that the ship was lunging back and forth in the ocean. A storm was brewing.

On another part of the ship, Team Rocket was arguing again.

"How are we going to tell the boss about this?" Meowth asked. "We were supposed to capture all of the Pokémon on the ship. And we have nothing!"

James gazed at his gold Pokéball and sighed. "We still have Magikarp!"

The ship lunged again. The golden ball flew out of James's hand.

"There goes next month's salary!" James cried, running after the ball.

"That's my money, too!" yelled Jessie, following him.

"*Meowth!* Wait for me!"

Team Rocket charged down the hallway. Another giant wave rocked the ship. The movement sent Jessie, James, and Meowth crashing into a wall.

They collapsed on the floor, motionless. They were knocked out.

Meanwhile, on deck, Misty and Brock watched the ship's captain and stewards round up the passengers.

"Stay calm, everyone," said the captain, an older man with a gray beard. "Just head for the lifeboats and you'll be fine."

"Lifeboats!" Misty said. "Brock, the ship is sinking."

The panicked passengers stormed toward the lifeboats.

"We've got to find Ash," Brock said.

"I think I know where to find him," Misty said. "Follow me!"

The ship rocked back and forth. Misty tried to keep her balance as she ran. Brock and Pikachu followed.

Wet and shivering from the rain, they burst through the door of the Pokémon trading room. The older trainer was gone, but Ash was there. He was holding a Poké Ball in his hands.

"I got my Butterfree back!" Ash said.

Crack! A thunderclap pierced the air.

"Ash, we've got to get out of here!" Misty said. "The ship is sinking."

The ship lurched again. The Poké Ball flew out of Ash's hands and rolled down the hallway.

"Butterfree!" Ash cried. He ran after it.

"Ash!" yelled Misty and Brock. They ran after Ash, with Pikachu right behind them.

Another wave crashed against the ship. Ash felt his feet fly out from under him. The four friends went flying against a wall. They fell to the ground, unconscious.

Above them, the storm still raged. The captain and crew were loading the last of the passengers onto the lifeboats.

"I think we've got everybody," the captain yelled over the roaring waves. "Let's go!"

The captain and crew lowered their lifeboat

into the churning water just in time. Behind them, the giant ship began to fill with water.

The S.S. *Anne* tossed in the water. A giant wave slammed against the ship.

The force of the wave pushed the ship upside down. The S.S. *Anne* was capsizing! Slowly, the ocean liner began to sink into the ocean.

Team Rocket was still inside.

And so were Ash, Misty, Brock, and Pikachu!

5

Go, Goldeen!

"Ash, wake up!" Misty pleaded.

"Pika pi!" added Pikachu.

Ash opened his eyes. Everything was a blur. Misty, Brock, and Pikachu slowly came into focus in front of him.

They were standing on the ceiling of the ship.

Ash rubbed his eyes and looked again. The floor of the ship was above them. He was sprawled out on the ceiling, just like his friends. They were upside down!

Panicked, Ash looked out the window.

Instead of blue sky, he saw murky, green water.

"The ship capsized! We sunk!" Ash said. "But why is there no water in here?"

"As long as there's air inside, it will take time to fill up with water," Misty explained. "We've got to stay calm."

Brock helped Ash to his feet. "You're right, but we can't waste any time. Let's look around."

The friends walked out of the room they were in and headed down a hallway. Dim emergency lights lined the floor above them. They followed the hall to an upside-down staircase that was covered with water.

"What are we supposed to do now?" Ash asked.

Misty looked thoughtful. "We're upside down. That means that the ship's deck is below us, and the ship's bottom is up above our heads!"

Ash pictured the upside-down ship in his mind. "I get it. To get out, we have to dive down to the deck, then swim back up to the surface."

Brock frowned. "But if we dive down to the deck and come across a dead end, then we're done for," he pointed out.

"No problem," Misty said. She pulled a Poké Ball from her knapsack. "Go, Goldeen!"

Misty threw the ball into the water. A fishlike Pokémon appeared. Goldeen was white and reddish-orange, with graceful, ruffled fins.

"Goldeen," the Pokémon said in a musical voice.

"Goldeen, dive down to the deck!" Misty ordered. "If you find a way off the ship, bring something back!"

"Goldeen," the Pokémon replied. Then it dove into the dark water.

It wasn't long before Goldeen came swimming back toward them. The Pokémon was pushing something with its head.

Something alive.

"Team Rocket?" Ash couldn't believe his eyes.

Jessie, James, and Meowth were soaked. Their eyes were closed. Goldeen pushed them up onto the ceiling in front of Ash.

The members of Team Rocket coughed and sputtered. They slowly opened their eyes. With a start, they leaped to their feet.

Jessie held out a Poké Ball.

"We've got you brats cornered!" she yelled.

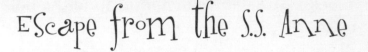

6

Escape from the S.S. Anne

Brock and Ash each grabbed a Poké Ball and faced Team Rocket.

"Let's go!" Ash cried.

Misty jumped between them.

"Wait!" she cried. "This is no time for a Pokémon battle. The ship is sinking!"

"You're right," Ash admitted.

Misty turned to Team Rocket. "What's more important — a Pokémon battle, or your life?"

"Good point," Jessie said, her voice cold.

"But this is just a temporary truce until we can get out of this horrible mess."

"Better believe it!" Ash said. Brock grunted in agreement.

James sneered. "So what's your brilliant plan for getting out of here?"

"Leave it to me," Misty said. "I built a model of the S.S. *Anne* once. I know the ship's structure. Since the way to the deck is blocked, we'll have to climb up to the bottom of the ship. We can cut a hole in the hull. That's how we'll escape."

Ash looked up. There was a hole in the floor above them that led to a dry upside-down stairway. It was the only way up.

"How are we supposed to climb up there?" Ash asked.

"Leave it to me," Brock said. He called on Onix, a giant rock Pokémon. Onix stretched its long, snakelike body up to the hole above them to form a staircase. Brock led the others up Onix's back and through the hole.

They emerged into another upside-down hallway. This hallway was high, but it was also dark. Ash called on Charmander to lead the way with its flaming tail.

"This corridor leads straight to the engine room," Misty explained. "The hull is thin there, so we should be able to cut our way through."

The group walked through the open engine room door, then abruptly stopped.

The engine room was on fire!

Ash looked across the room. There was a door on the other side of the room. The flames hadn't reached the door — yet.

"Bulbasaur! I choose you!" Ash called.

The blue-green Pokémon appeared. Ash commanded it to use its Vine Whip to create a bridge across the flames. Then Ash led the others across the vines like they were tightropes.

"We did it!" Misty said when

they were all safely across. "Now all we have to do is break through the hull."

"I can have Charmander burn through the hull of the ship with its flame," Ash suggested.

"Good idea," Misty said. "But first, everyone grab hold of a Water Pokémon. We'll need them to swim to the surface."

Water Pokémon were Misty's specialty. She released Goldeen from its Poké Ball, and gave Brock a Starmie. Then Misty tied one end of a rope around her waist. She tied the other end around Goldeen.

Following her lead, Ash tied himself and Pikachu to Squirtle. Brock tied himself to Starmie.

"Charmander!" Ash commanded. "Burn a hole in the hull with your flame!"

The Pokémon obeyed. It opened its mouth wide and began to burn a wide, square hole in the metal above them.

Jessie looked panicked. "Water Pokémon? We don't have any Water Pokémon."

James snickered. He held out his golden

Poké Ball. "You made fun of me before. But
now Magikarp will prove its worth."

James threw the Poké Ball, and
Magikarp appeared. Team Rocket tied
themselves to the Pokémon.

Above them, Charmander's flame was
burning through the hull. The metal came
crashing down onto the floor. Seawater
poured through the hole, flooding the
chamber.

Goldeen, Squirtle, and Starmie swam up

the torrent of water and through the hole. Ash, Misty, Brock, and Pikachu closed their eyes and held their breath as the water covered them. They held on tightly to the ropes. It was all up to the Pokémon now.

Team Rocket watched as their rivals were carried to safety.

"Let's go, Magikarp!" James commanded.

"Magikarp," the Pokémon gulped. It flapped its fins helplessly.

"Don't tell me that fish can't swim!" Jessie said angrily.

Seawater was filling the chamber. Team Rocket struggled against the current. They tried to swim up to the hole.

It was no use. The water pushed them back into the sinking ship.

"We're doomed!" Meowth cried.

7

Dragon Rage!

Sunlight blinded Ash's eyes as Squirtle pulled him to the ocean's surface. Gasping for air, Ash looked around him. Pikachu, Misty, and Brock were all safe.

Brock was hanging on to a large chunk of fiberglass. The piece of the S.S. *Anne* had broken off when the ship sank. Now it float-ed in the ocean like a raft.

"Over here!" Brock called.

Ash, Pikachu, and Squirtle climbed aboard. Misty and Goldeen were right behind them. Misty and Ash recalled their

Water Pokémon. Then they all sprawled out on the raft, exhausted.

Ash scanned the calm ocean waters. Small pieces of debris bobbed in the water, but nothing else. "Team Rocket still hasn't surfaced," he remarked. "I wonder if they're trapped inside."

"There's nothing we can do," Brock said, "except try to find some dry land."

Ash looked all around him. There was nothing but blue sky and green ocean in sight. He sent his Pidgeotto in search of dry land. Ash watched as the birdlike Pokémon disappeared over the horizon.

Ash slumped down on the raft. "This could take awhile," he said.

"Maybe not," Misty said.

In an instant, Pidgeotto was flying back. It had a rope in its beak. It was pulling along a small metal piece of the ship. Clinging to the metal were Jessie, James, and Meowth. Magikarp flopped in the water beside them.

"Team Rocket!" Ash exclaimed. "Those guys must have nine lives."

"*Meowth!* You can say that again," said the catlike Pokémon, spitting water from its mouth. Meowth hopped onto the raft.

Jessie and James opened their eyes and crawled aboard.

"Prepare for trouble," said Jessie weakly.

"Make it double," moaned James.

Misty sighed. "You two are too much."

Jessie groaned. "We almost drowned, thanks to that useless Magikarp of yours, James."

"You're right," James admitted. He glared at the Pokémon. "Magikarp, you good-for-nothing fish! I don't want to be your master anymore!"

James pushed Magikarp off the raft and into the sea. The Pokémon bobbed up and down on the waves.

"Good riddance!" Meowth said.

"I feel kind of sorry for it," Misty said.

"*Magikarp. Magikarp.*" The Pokémon

flapped its fins furiously. Suddenly, Magikarp began to glow with a white light. Then the light exploded in a brilliant flash.

Ash was blinded for a split second. When he looked out at the water again, Magikarp was gone.

In its place was a huge Pokémon. Ash thought it must have been two stories tall. The Pokémon looked like a sea serpent covered in shiny blue scales. It had four long fangs. Feathery gills framed its face.

"Magikarp has evolved into Gyarados!" Misty exclaimed.

Ash's handheld computer, Dexter the Pokédex, spoke. "Gyarados has a vicious temper. Its fangs can crush stones and its scales are harder than steel."

Gyarados roared loudly.

James faced the Pokémon. "I'm James, your master. Obey me!"

Gyarados roared angrily. James screamed in fear.

"What should we do?" Ash asked.

Misty threw a Poké Ball into the water. "Goldeen! Starmie! Staryu!" she called out.

Goldeen and the two star-shaped

Pokémon appeared.

"How will you battle Gyarados?" Brock asked.

Misty threw a rope to each of the Pokémon. "My battle strategy is — RUN!" Misty yelled.

Goldeen, Starmie, and Staryu pulled the raft through the water. They were whizzing through the sea, but they were no match for Gyarados. The Pokémon was right behind them.

Suddenly, Gyarados stopped. It roared loudly.

"What's it doing?" Ash asked, looking behind him.

Misty's face clouded. "Sailors tell terrible stories about Gyarados. I think this might be . . . Dragon Rage."

"Dragon Rage?" the others asked in surprise.

The water began to churn. Four wild Gyarados raised their long necks above the water and joined James's Gyarados. The five sea serpents formed a straight line. Then the giant Pokémon began weaving in between one another like they were doing a crazy dance.

"It *is* Dragon Rage!" Misty cried. "Gyarados's ultimate attack!"

The five Gyarados spun in circles. The water around them began to form a spiral. Faster and faster swam the Gyarados. The water spiral got bigger and bigger.

Soon the circle of water began to rise into the sky.

The Gyarados were making a water cyclone!

Ash had never seen anything like it. The cyclone looked like a tornado made out of water. The cyclone whipped around furiously in front of them.

The water cyclone began to travel in a straight path toward the raft.

"Here it comes!" Ash yelled.

There was no escape.

Ash grabbed Pikachu's hand. "Hold on tight!" Ash called out over the roar of the raging water.

Ash felt Misty grab his other hand. Brock grabbed hold of Misty and Pikachu. The friends formed a circle and braced for the cyclone to hit.

The spiraling water funnel crashed into the raft. Ash felt himself being pulled into the cyclone. The cold water stung his face.

The friends twirled around and around in the center of the cyclone. Ash felt Pikachu's hand slip from his. Misty's hand was slipping away too.

"Don't let go!" Ash yelled. But it was too late. Ash lost his grip. The force of the cyclone pulled him away from his friends. Ash went flying into the sky.

Ash plummeted back down into the ocean. His body slammed into the water.

Then his world went black.

8

Stranded

"Where am I?" Ash asked groggily. His voice was hoarse. His head was pounding. His arms were covered with sand.

Sand? Ash opened his eyes. He was on a white, sandy beach. Palm trees and green leafy plants dotted the shoreline.

Ash began to panic. The last thing he remembered was losing his friends. Where were they?

Ash scrambled to his feet. He looked around. There was Misty, sprawled out on the sand just a few feet away. Brock was lying next to her, his body a crumpled heap.

"Misty! Brock! Wake up!" Ash shook his friends.

Misty groaned and opened her eyes. Brock did the same.

"How did we get here?" Misty asked.

Brock rubbed his head. "Yeah, how did we survive that cyclone?"

"We were lucky," Ash said. He nervously scanned the beach. "Or at least I think we were lucky. I don't see Pikachu anywhere."

"That's not all we're missing," Misty said. She pointed to Ash's belt.

Ash reached down. Two of his Poké Balls were attached. But three were missing.

"My Pokémon are gone!" Ash cried.

On the other side of the island, Jessie and James had landed in a sand dune. The two Pokémon thieves crawled out of the sand.

"We've survived again!" Jessie exclaimed.

"We're completely invincible!" James added.

Jessie and James waited for Meowth to join in. But the beach was quiet.

"Oh no!" Jessie cried.

"Meowth is gone!" James said.

Panicked, Jessie looked down at her uniform. "Oh no! I've lost the Poké Ball with the Ekans I got for my birthday!"

James checked his uniform. "The Poké Ball with my Koffing is gone, too!"

Jessie and James looked at each other in despair. Tears poured from their eyes. "What happened to our Pokémon?" they cried out.

There was no answer.

9

Pokémon on their own

On another part of the island, Pikachu walked along a sandy beach. It wasn't hurt. But it was a little afraid. After the cyclone hit, Pikachu was separated from Ash. Now it couldn't find Ash anywhere.

Pikachu saw red-and-white objects gleaming in the sand. It ran over to see what they were.

Ash's Poké Balls!

Excited, Pikachu touched each of the Poké Balls. They opened up. White light flashed from each one.

First, Charmander appeared. Then Bulbasaur. Then Squirtle.

"Pika, Pika!" Pikachu said. Even though each Pokémon spoke its own language, they could understand one another. The other Pokémon knew that Pikachu was saying, *"Are you all okay?"*

"I'm all right," said Charmander, a little weakly.

"I've felt better!" said Squirtle.

Bulbasaur was more stubborn. *"I'm just fine,"* it said.

Squirtle looked around the beach. *"Where are we?"* asked the Water Pokémon.

"I don't know," Pikachu said. *"But I think we should try to find Ash."*

"Okay," the others agreed.

Pikachu found a path that led away from the beach. The other Pokémon followed Pikachu through the sand.

Tall green plants lined the path. Palm trees and fruit trees rose above them.

For awhile, the Pokémon walked in silence. Then the sun began to sink behind the trees.

Charmander moved to the head of the group and lit up the growing darkness with its flaming tail. The light was comforting. Even so, Pikachu was getting nervous.

"I don't see Ash and those guys anywhere," Pikachu said.

"Maybe they all got eaten by wild Pokémon," Squirtle joked. It chomped its teeth and laughed.

Pikachu didn't like Squirtle's joke. *"Don't say things like that,"* Pikachu scolded.

Squirtle frowned. *"Sorry."*

Bulbasaur looked sad, too. *"Maybe Ash forgot about us."*

"Ash would never do that!" Pikachu protested.

Squirtle nodded. *"You're right. He's not like that."*

Bulbasaur didn't seem convinced. *"Maybe,"* it said.

A rustling in the plants in front of them made Pikachu look up. Something jumped out at them.

It was Meowth!

"Surrender now or prepare to fight!" Meowth said.

Bulbasaur, Squirtle, and Charmander jumped a little. Pikachu turned to them.

"Don't worry, it's just Meowth," it said.

The Pokémon relaxed.

"I guess Team Rocket's motto is losing its impact," Meowth said. "That's no big deal. I've got reinforcements." He pointed to a rocky ledge behind him.

Ekans, a purple snakelike Pokémon, was curled up on the rock. Koffing, a

Poison-Gas Pokémon, was floating next to Ekans.

"Go get 'em!" Meowth ordered.

Ekans and Koffing didn't move.

"You not master," Ekans hissed. *"I only obey master."*

Meowth stomped its foot on the ground. "Come on, we're all bad guys here! We don't need masters to tell us to do bad stuff!"

"Pokémon not bad guys," Ekans said. *"Pokémon only do bad things because master bad."*

"That's right!" Koffing huffed in its deep voice.

"You're wrong! My master's not here and I'm still a bad guy," Meowth said angrily. It turned to fight Pikachu, but then stopped in its tracks. Pikachu, Bulbasaur, Squirtle, and Charmander had formed a circle around it.

"You sure you want to fight against all of us?" Pikachu asked.

Meowth smiled nervously. "Oh, I guess we could call it a draw."

"Not good enough," Pikachu said.

"*Bulbasaur, you know what to do.*"

Bulbasaur nodded and sent vines flying out of the plant bulb on its back. The vines lashed around Meowth, tying it tightly.

"*We can't take any chances,*" Pikachu said.

Squirtle's stomach rumbled. "*Squirtle hungry,*" it said.

"*Me too,*" said Pikachu. "*Let's set up camp.*"

Charmander gathered sticks and made a small campfire. The other Pokémon gathered fruit from the trees. Then they sat around the campfire, munching on the food.

"*What were you guys doing?*" Pikachu asked Ekans and Koffing.

"*Looking for masters,*" Ekans hissed.

"*Ours is gone, too,*" said Squirtle.

Bulbasaur frowned. "*He's abandoned us.*"

"*Abandoned?*" asked Ekans. "*Maybe us, too!*"

Pikachu shook its head. "*No, you're all wrong!*" It knew Ash would never abandon them.

The Pokémon continued to munch on their food. They all felt a little sad. The sound of crunching filled the night air.

Suddenly, another sound echoed around them — a low, rumbling sound. The ground beneath them began to shake.

Pikachu looked up. There, towering above the trees, was a foot.

A giant foot.

The Pokémon jumped up. Attached to

the foot was a gray Pokémon, a Rhydon. It looked like a rhinoceros that walked on two legs. It had a large horn in the middle of its forehead.

Pikachu had seen a Rhydon before. But never one this big. It was as big as the skyscrapers in Celadon City.

The Rhydon roared loudly. It took another step. It was coming for the Pokémon!

"Let's get out of here!" Charmander yelled.

The Pokémon began to run down the path.

"Hey, what about me?" Meowth cried. "I'm all tied up here!"

The oversized Rhydon was getting closer. Pikachu thought for a split second. Then it ran back and untied Meowth.

"I could have done it myself," Meowth said.

Normally, Pikachu would have given Meowth a good shock. But there was no time.

Pikachu ran down the path after its friends. Meowth followed right behind.

Up ahead, Pikachu saw a small cave.

"In there! In there!" Pikachu cried.

The Pokémon ran into the cave. They huddled together in fear.

Rhydon roared again.

Stomp! Stomp!

The ground shook.

Pikachu watched as a big gray foot stomped down in front of the cave. Then the foot lifted up. It stomped down again.

Rhydon walked right past the cave.

They were safe — for now.

"Charmander tired," said the Fire Pokémon wearily.

"Me too," said Squirtle.

"Let's sleep here," said Pikachu. *"We can find Ash in the morning."*

"Find masters," Ekans hissed. The big snakelike Pokémon uncoiled its body and formed a large circle. The other Pokémon curled up inside the circle, exhausted.

But Pikachu couldn't fall asleep right away. As long as that big Pokémon was out there, they weren't safe.

And neither was Ash.

Flying Pokémon Attack!

10

"Run, Ash, run!" Misty cried.

Ash didn't need Misty to tell him what to do. He was already running for his life.

All afternoon Ash, Misty, and Brock had searched the island, looking for Pikachu and the other Pokémon. There was no trace of them on the quiet island.

But as soon as the sun went down, things got crazy. A giant, flying Pokémon appeared in the sky. It was the legendary Pokémon, Zapdos. Its body glowed with golden light. Its feathers looked like jagged knives. Flashes like lightning bolts sparked from its wings.

But there was something strange about this Zapdos. It was huge — bigger than a jet plane.

Ash had stared at the amazing sight for a second. Then the super-sized Zapdos let out a piercing cry. It dove through the sky — right at them!

Ash's feet pounded against the sandy

ground. His heart beat furiously in his chest.

The giant bird shrieked. Ash looked up. It was right above them!

Brock grabbed Ash's sleeve and pulled him off the path. Misty was already running ahead of them. The three friends dove under a leafy bush.

The Zapdos shrieked again. Ash held his breath. The bird's cries were growing fainter.

It was flying away.

They had escaped!

"Ash, this place is really dangerous," Brock said.

Misty nodded. "Who knows what else is out there?"

"We should find a place to crash for the night," Brock said.

"You're right," Ash agreed. He stepped back onto the path and looked into the night sky.

"Be careful, Pikachu — all of you," Ash said softly.

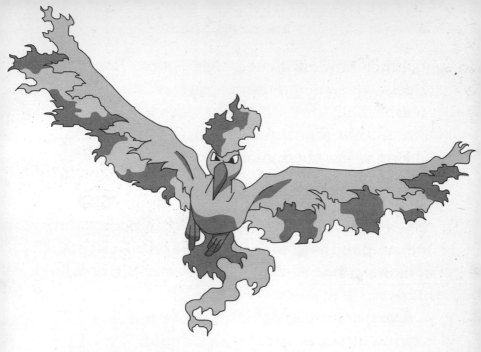

On the other side of the island, another piercing cry filled the night air.

It was Jessie and James. They were screaming in terror.

Another giant Flying Pokémon was on the attack — a Moltres. The body of this red-orange bird was surrounded by flames.

Jessie and James ran from the combination Fire and Flying Pokémon. Moltres swooped down, opened its beak, and blew a stream of bright red flames right at them.

The flames licked at Team Rocket's heels. Jessie and James ran as fast as they could.

Up ahead, Jessie spotted something gleaming in the moonlight.

It was a phone booth.

"Quick!" Jessie said. "Inside."

Jessie and James ran into the booth and closed the door. Moltres cried out overhead. The Pokémon flew in a circle over the booth. Then it flew away.

"A phone booth? On a deserted island?" James thought he was dreaming.

"Who cares how it got here?" Jessie said. "Now we can call for help."

James pulled out his empty pockets. "We could, if we had money. But I spent every cent on Magikarp, remember?"

"If I ever hear that name again —" Jessie fumed angrily. Then she composed herself. "At least we'll be safe for the night," she said.

"Yes," said James. "But who knows what we'll find out there in the morning?"

11

Runaway Train!

"Pika?" Pikachu woke up and rubbed its eyes. The morning sun was shining outside the cave. Bulbasaur, Squirtle, Charmander, Ekans, Koffing, and Meowth were all waking up.

"Let's go everybody," Pikachu said. *"We can look for Ash now."*

Charmander peeked outside the cave. *"What if there's big Pokémon out there?"*

Pikachu stepped into the sunlight. It looked out into the trees.

"The coast is clear," Pikachu said.

The other Pokémon followed Pikachu out of the cave. They walked into the leafy island jungle.

"Ash! Ash! Where are you?" Pikachu cried.

"Jessie! James!" Meowth called out.

Bulbasaur sighed. *"We'll never find them,"* it said sadly.

Suddenly, Squirtle stopped in its tracks.

"Uh, I think we found something," Squirtle said, pointing. *"Look!"*

Pikachu turned around. There was another giant Pokémon! It had its back to them.

This one looked like a giant turtle. Its shell was made of hard armor. Two metal water cannons protruded from each shoulder.

"Is that a relative of yours, Squirtle?" Charmander asked.

"This is Squirtle's most evolved form — a Blastoise," Meowth explained.

Pikachu turned to Squirtle. *"Go ask it for directions."*

"All right. I'll try," Squirtle said bravely.

Squirtle walked up behind Blastoise. It cleared its throat and tried to act calm. *"Yo, brother,"* Squirtle said.

Blastoise slowly turned around. It studied Squirtle with its piercing gaze.

"Uh, nice weather we're having," Squirtle said.

Blastoise roared. It lifted a giant foot and stomped toward the Pokémon.

"Let's get out of here!" Pikachu said. The Pokémon ran down the nearest path. The Blastoise was big, but it was slow. It gave up the chase.

"We made it!" said Meowth.

"Not so fast," said Pikachu. *"Look!"*

They had run from the Blastoise — right into another giant Pokémon!

This Pokémon was munching on plants. It looked like a big

dinosaur with blue skin. It had green leaves growing out of its back. A large flower with pink petals sprouted from between the leaves.

"That's a Venusaur — evolved from an Ivysaur that evolved from a Bulbasaur," Meowth explained.

"Awesome!" Squirtle said. *"Bulbasaur, talk to it. You guys are like family!"*

Bulbasaur shook its head. *"No way! Just call me an orphan. I don't have any family."*

"Come on, dude," Squirtle prodded. *"If I had to do it, so do you."*

At the sound of their voices, the Venusaur looked up at the Pokémon. It let out a loud roar. Then it charged at them.

"Oh no! Not again!" Bulbasaur complained.

Bulbasaur ran through the trees. The other Pokémon followed right behind.

Nearby, Team Rocket was waking up in the cramped phone booth.

James stretched and stepped outside. "What do we do now?" he asked.

Jessie stepped out next to him. A thick, black telephone cable was attached to the phone booth. It ran along the ground as far as Jessie could see.

"This cable must lead to the phone company," Jessie said. "The people there can help us get off the island."

"What are we waiting for?" James asked.

Jessie and James hopped back into the phone booth. They grabbed hold of the phone cable and began pulling it. They dragged themselves — and the phone booth — bit by bit.

"We'll be safe if we stay in the phone booth," Jessie said.

James huffed and puffed. "Jessie, hauling this phone booth is exhausting," he whined after a few yards.

71

"Well, you could use a good workout," Jessie snapped.

A low rumbling sound followed. James looked out of the phone booth.

A Pokémon was walking toward them. Jessie and James saw the top of its yellow head over the horizon.

"Is that a mirage?" James asked.

"It's Pikachu!" Jessie cried. "And it doesn't even see us."

"So we'll have no trouble catching it." James grinned. "Maybe this island isn't so bad after all."

They leaped out of the phone booth, ready to tie up Pikachu with the cable.

The Pikachu got closer and closer. It wasn't long before Jessie and James saw that this Pikachu wasn't Ash's Pikachu after all.

It was gigantic!

"It *is* a mirage," Jessie said.

"A really *big* mirage," James answered.

The enormous Pikachu stomped up to the phone booth. It lifted a huge, yellow foot above them.

"It's *Big*-achu!" they yelled. Jessie grabbed James's arm and pulled him out of the way.

Stomp! The giant Pikachu's foot came crashing down on the booth. The phone booth smashed into pieces. The Pikachu stomped away, ignoring Team Rocket.

"My, that was a close call," James said.

"This is no time for jokes, James," Jessie said. "We've got to find a way off this island!"

Jessie started running, still following the phone cable. James was right behind her.

Suddenly, Jessie stopped in her tracks. The ground she was standing on was shaking.

Jessie and James looked behind them.

Another giant Pokémon was running after them. This Pokémon looked like a giant insect that walked on two legs. Its long arms ended in sharp, curved swords. It was a Kabutops. Normally, Kabutops was

only four-foot-three, but this one was fifty feet tall!

"This is a nightmare!" Jessie screamed.

Jessie and James ran along the cable. Kabutops stomped behind them, swiping at them with its claws.

Up ahead, Jessie saw some railroad tracks. An old mining cart sat on the tracks. It looked like an open wagon on wheels. It had handles in the middle so that it could be propelled along the tracks.

"Let's hop in and make a run for it!" Jessie yelled.

Jessie and James jumped into the cart. They each grabbed a handle and began pumping furiously. The cart moved quickly along the tracks.

But the telephone cable had somehow become attached to the wheels of the wagon. Kabutops grabbed the cable and started pulling the cart toward it.

"Oh no!" James screamed.

"Let's hit the brake and run for it!" Jessie suggested.

The brake was a lever on the floor of the

cart. Jessie grabbed the brake.

It broke in two pieces.

Without the brake, the mining cart sped forward. Kabutops became tangled in the cable and went crashing to the ground. But the mining cart was going so fast it couldn't be slowed down. Kabutops was dragged along the tracks behind the cart.

"Runaway train!" James cried.

12

Giant Pokémon on the Loose!

"So far so good," Brock said. "No sign of any more giant Pokémon."

Ash sighed. "There's no sign of Pikachu and the others, either," he said sadly. "Where could they all have gone?"

"Don't worry, Ash," Misty said. "We'll find them."

Ash, Misty, and Brock were searching the island for Pikachu and the other Pokémon. They had been walking all morning along a sandy path. Now the path ended at a stone bridge.

Ash stepped onto the bridge. He looked below. A railroad track crossed underneath them.

"I wonder where that leads?" Ash wondered.

Suddenly, the bridge began to shake.

"Uh-oh," Misty said. "That sounds like a giant Pokémon to me."

Stomp. Stomp. Stomp. It was getting closer.

"We'd better run for it," Brock said.

"Right," Ash agreed. He started to run, then skidded to a stop.

A giant Pokémon emerged from the trees next to the railroad tracks. This Pokémon was bright yellow. It had pointy ears and a lightning bolt-shaped tail.

"Pikachu!" Ash cried.

"Jumbo-sized!" Brock added.

The giant Pikachu stomped down the railroad tracks. It was headed right for them.

Before Ash could react, the bridge began to shake again. Now there was another noise. This was a loud, rumbling sound.

A cloud of dust sped down the railroad tracks behind Pikachu.

The dust cloud got closer. Ash could make out a mining cart. Jessie and James were inside it.

Behind the mining cart was another giant Pokémon — a Kabutops. It was tangled up in a cable. The cart was dragging the giant Pokémon along the tracks.

"Look out!" Jessie yelled.

The mining cart sped between the giant Pikachu's legs. The Pikachu got tangled up in the cable, too. It crashed on top of the Kabutops.

The crash rocked the stone bridge. The bridge began to crumble!

It was breaking apart!

Ash screamed as the bridge gave way beneath him. He, Misty, and Brock fell through the bridge.

And landed in the cart!

"Now we've got you just where we want you," Jessie said.

"Will you cut it out!" Misty yelled. "Look!"

There was a giant Blastoise. A giant Venusaur. A giant Rhydon. The giant Zapdos and Moltres were flying in the air.

The giant Pokémon were chasing Ash's Pikachu and the other normal-sized Pokémon. They were all running toward the railroad tracks.

"We've got to help them!" Ash cried.

"Ash!" Misty interrupted. "Up ahead!"

Ash turned. In front of them, the track turned into a giant loop that rose high in the sky.

They weren't on railroad tracks at all.

They were on roller coaster tracks!

"Hold on tight!" Brock called out.

Ash grabbed the sides of the cart and closed his eyes. The cart sped up one side of the loop. In a flash, they were upside down. Then they went back down the loop. They were back on the tracks again.

Ash opened his eyes. They had made it!

"What about Pikachu?" Ash remembered suddenly.

Ash looked to the side. The normal-sized

Pokémon were running toward the cart. The giant Pokémon were right behind them.

"Jump in!" Ash called out.

Pikachu took a flying leap and landed in Ash's arms. Brock caught Squirtle and Bulbasaur. Misty caught Charmander.

Ekans, Koffing, and Meowth jumped in next. They had all made it!

Ash looked behind them. Blastoise, Venosaur, and Rhydon thundered down the track.

"The giant Pokémon are still after us," Ash said. "They're right behind us!"

James looked at the giant Pokémon. "These last few days, Team Rocket has survived every danger," James said. "Based on our recent run of luck, I would say that right about now the cable will snap."

At James's words, the giant Pokémon got tangled in the cable. The tiny cart couldn't pull so many giant Pokémon. The cable strained with the weight. Then it snapped.

"Next, we'll be hurtled into the air," James said.

The snapping cable acted like a catapult. Ash braced himself as the railroad cart went flying into the air.

"And finally, we'll crash into something and fall into the water," James said.

The cart turned upside down in midair. The giant Zapdos was right above them. The bottom of the cart struck one of Zapdos's sharp wings. The cart snapped in two.

Jessie, James, and their Pokémon went flying off in one direction.

"This is so cool!" Ash said. "I love theme parks!"

Misty groaned. "Ash, you are unbelievable."

Ash began to climb out of the lagoon. The giant Pokémon were falling apart. They didn't look so scary anymore.

"I guess there's nothing more to do here," Ash said. "Where should we go next?"

"Pikachu," Pikachu said. *"Pika pika."*

Ash laughed.

"What did it say?" Misty asked.

"Pikachu said we could go anywhere — except on a cruise," Ash said.

The friends all laughed. They climbed onto the shore, glad that this adventure was over.

Of course, they couldn't wait for the next one!

About the Author

Tracey West has been writing books for more than ten years. When she's not playing the blue version of the Pokémon game (she started with a Squirtle), she enjoys reading comic books, watching cartoons, and taking long walks in the woods (looking for wild Pokémon). She lives in a small town in New York with her family and pets.

coming soon...

POKÉMON #3
Attack of the Prehistoric Pokémon

Ash, Misty, Brock, and Pikachu go on a Pokémon fossil dig. Things get explosive when Team Rocket accidentally wakes up some cranky ancient Pokémon — including a flying Aerodactyl! Then Ash finds a mysterious Pokémon egg. Could it hold a brand-new Pokémon?

catch it in September!